THE WATER BABIES

by
Charles Kingsley

Retold by Jane Carruth

Illustrated by
Anne Grahame Johnstone

AWARD PUBLICATIONS LIMITED

Once upon a time there was a little chimney-sweep called Tom. Tom couldn't read or write and he didn't care much about that. He was always dirty because he never washed and he didn't care about that either. What he did mind was when his master beat him every day of his life, and when the soot got in his eyes and made them smart and sting.

Tom's master was Mr Grimes, the meanest, cruellest bully in the whole land. Mr Grimes spent all the money Tom earned for him on himself and on tobacco for his pipe.

One day Mr Grimes got a new customer which greatly pleased him, especially as his new customer was Sir John of Hall Place – a great big house in the country with so many chimneys to sweep you couldn't count them.

And so, early the next morning, Tom and his master set out, Grimes riding the donkey in front and Tom with the brushes walking behind.

Tom had never been so far into the country before and longed to stop, but he did not dare. And, after a while, they caught up with a tall, handsome woman in a crimson petticoat. She had a grey shawl over her head and her eyes were bright. When Grimes invited her to ride behind him on his donkey, she said, "I'll walk with your boy!".

And so she did. She talked to Tom about himself until he quite lost his heart to her – never guessing that she was a fairy – when suddenly and without warning she vanished from sight!

When they reached the big house the gates were opened by a keeper and they were sent round to the back door.

The housekeeper came and gave Grimes orders as to what he might and might not do before taking them into a fine, big room. Then, after a kick from his master which sent him into the grate, Tom started up his first chimney.

Tom stopped counting all the chimneys he swept that morning. In the end, he was so tired that he lost his way among them and finally came down the wrong one.

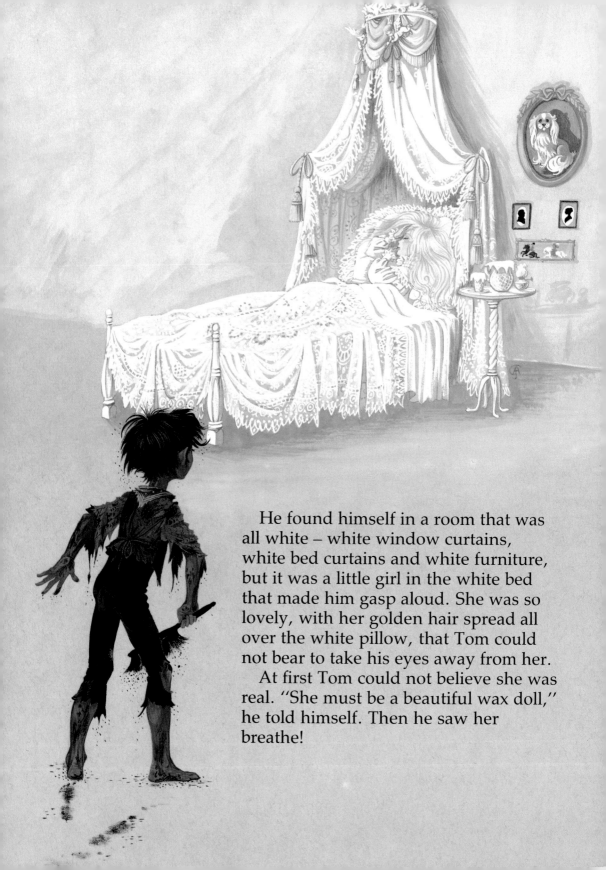

He found himself in a room that was all white – white window curtains, white bed curtains and white furniture, but it was a little girl in the white bed that made him gasp aloud. She was so lovely, with her golden hair spread all over the white pillow, that Tom could not bear to take his eyes away from her.

At first Tom could not believe she was real. "She must be a beautiful wax doll," he told himself. Then he saw her breathe!

Poor Tom. His wonder at seeing the little girl in white was suddenly changed to horror as he caught sight of himself in her long mirror. Was that dirty, black, ragged figure Tom, the little chimney-sweep? It must be. Tom turned away quickly, tears of shame in his eyes, with only one desire. He must escape up the chimney again before she woke up and saw him.

Then the little girl opened her eyes and when she saw dirty Tom she began to scream. In rushed her old nurse and tried to grab him, but Tom was too quick for her. He was out of the open window in a flash and clambering down the spreading tree underneath.

Once free of the house Tom took to his heels, with shouts of "Stop thief!" ringing in his ears.

"After him! After him!" shouted
Sir John, and after him they went:
the gardener, the keeper,
the dairymaid, the groom,
and others besides,
shouting and yelling as
Tom ducked and dodged.

He ran across the park as if
a pack of hounds were after him,
struggling for breath, his heart
pounding.

Once free of the great park,
he made for the woods just as any
hunted animal might do. But the
woods offered him no proper place
to hide and the fallen branches
slowed him down.

The shouts of his pursuers were
growing faint as Tom left the woods
for the vast lonely moors that
stretched endlessly before him.

The rough bracken and heather tore at Tom's bare feet as he ran on, and when he could no longer run, he slowed down to a walk. Soon he found he was climbing and he stopped every now and then to draw breath, telling himself, "I'm free of them at last. They will never catch me now. If only I had something to eat," he thought, "I could keep on for ever and ever."

And all the time he was climbing he had no idea that not far behind was the fairy he had lost his heart to early that morning.

Tom's poor head was starting to spin and he began to imagine that he could hear the sound of church bells ringing a long, long way off. "If there is a church there should be people," he said to himself. "And it is people I need – or just one kind person to give me shelter and something to eat and some water to drink."

He was certain he had lost his pursuers long ago. He was certain, too, that now he would never go back. He had seen the last of his cruel master that morning. Never again would he be the poor little chimney-sweep working for Mr Grimes.

Now Tom had reached the top of the mountain, and there was nowhere for him to go but to begin climbing down.

Bravely, Tom set out to do just that. Below, he could see a deep green valley and woods, and through the woods a clear silver stream. Tom longed to reach the stream and put his hot, sore feet in its cool water.

The valley, the woods and the stream looked a hundred miles away to Tom as he began the long, dangerous climb down, and when he found himself on top of a high cliff, he hung there for a moment. Then glancing downwards over his shoulder, he thought he spied a little cottage set in a garden, and his friend in the crimson petticoat!

For Tom there was now no turning back and he was terribly tired and dizzy by the time he reached the valley. So he lay down on the grass and fell fast asleep. After a while he opened his eyes, got up, and stumbled away along a narrow path that led to the prettiest cottage in the world.

The door was open and Tom peeped into the room, too shy to enter. In a high-backed chair sat an old woman with a black silk handkerchief tied over her clean white cap, and at her feet an old ginger cat.

"That old lady must be a teacher," Tom decided, seeing that opposite her on wooden benches were seated two rows of well-scrubbed children.

All the clean, rosy children saw Tom and began to stare at his dirty, black figure. Some of the boys started to laugh and some of the little girls looked frightened.

"Who are you and what do you want?" cried the old woman. When poor Tom remained silent, she cried again:

"I can see what you are. You are a sweep. Go away! I don't want any chimney-sweeps here!"

"I only want a drink of water," Tom said weakly.

"You can get water in the stream," replied the woman sharply. "Off with you!"

"But I – I can't get there," Tom protested. "I'm too hungry and thirsty to take another step," and he sank down on the doorstep.

Then the old lady looked at him
more closely through her spectacles.

"The boy is sick," she declared at
last. She got up and went over to
him. "I'll not give you water," she
went on, "I'll give you milk. That
will be better for you."

The children were silent now, and
the boys stopped laughing at Tom
as their teacher went off to get the
milk and some bread.

As soon as Tom had drunk the
milk he began to feel better. But
when he tried to get up he was so
faint that the old lady had to help
him to his feet.

She led him to the barn outside,
saying, "Rest on the hay and when
school is over I'll come back." Then she
went away, expecting Tom to fall asleep.

Tom did not fall asleep after all. He tossed and turned on the soft sweet hay, his heart filled with longing for the cool waters of the river. Then, only half-asleep, he began thinking of the beautiful little girl in the wonderful white room and how he had terrified her because he was so dirty. He began to wish that he was clean. "I must be clean," he told himself. "I must wash in the river."

Tom had no idea how he got into the meadow, but all of a sudden he was there with the river just in front of him. He dipped his hand in the water and found it cool and refreshing. So he quickly pulled off all his old rags and put his hot feet into the water. Into the river he went, deeper and deeper.

All this time he had no idea that the fairy was there – at first behind him as he left the barn, and then in front of him. She entered the river before he did and her crimson petticoat floated away from her and the white waterlilies floated round her head.

Then all the water-fairies came to give her a royal welcome home. They took her away to the bottom of the river, rejoicing that their queen was back among them once again.

"Where have you been?" the fairies asked their queen at last. "We have missed you!"

"I have been doing all I can to help those who will not help themselves," she told them, "and I have brought you a present, a new little brother."

This made the fairies so happy that they laughed for joy, but then the queen said that they must not play with him until he had learned to be good.

"He must not see you, but you must look after him and keep him from harm!" the queen told the fairies.

Now, when Tom went into the river he did not know that he was going to become a water baby. But that is just what happened to him. There he was, swimming about, no more than pencil-high!

Of course he had no idea that it was the fairies who had turned him into a water baby. All he knew was that he liked swimming about in the water and he liked being clean!

At first Tom was very happy being a water baby. There were so many strange creatures to watch or tease or chase. In the water-forest some of the oddest were the water-monkeys and the water-squirrels, all with six legs!

Then Tom grew lonely. He wanted to meet other water babies and though he searched and searched he could not find any. At last he did find a kind of a playmate; not a water baby but a crusty old lobster who was willing to talk to Tom.

"I wish I could find a water baby," Tom confided to him, as they sat in a hole in the rocks. "I mean to go on looking until I do."

Poor Tom! The fairies and water babies were all round him but he was not allowed to see them.

So Tom went on searching for water babies and teasing all the sea-creatures to amuse himself, and, as he swam up and down, he met with an adventure which nearly put an end to him! It all began when he found himself among some rocks.

Do you remember the little girl in the white room? Her name was Ellie. And one day Ellie and an old professor, who was staying with her father, were exploring the rocks. The old professor was fishing with his net under the weeds, hoping to catch something strange and pretty to show little Ellie. Instead, he caught poor Tom. Tom got the fright of his life. But when the professor began prodding him, his fright turned to rage and he bit the old man's finger. And, very much annoyed, the professor dropped him in the weeds, and Tom dived into the water and was gone in a flash.

After his narrow escape, Tom did meet a water baby and helped him plant a rock-garden of seaweeds and anemones. As a reward, he was allowed to meet all the others.

"You must be good," they warned him. "We hear Mrs Bedonebyasyoudid is coming on Friday." But Tom didn't listen to them.

Early on Friday morning, Mrs Bedonebyasyoudid arrived. She had a black bonnet and shawl and a pair of big green spectacles on her long hooked nose. When all the water babies were lined up in front of her she gave them sea-cake and sea-toffee and other nice things out of her basket. But when it was Tom's turn, instead of giving him a delicious sea-cake, she popped a cold, hard pebble into his mouth, because he had put pebbles in the sea-anemones' mouths to make them think they had caught some food.

Tom was sorry for what he had done and when on Sunday a pretty lady called Mrs Doasyouwouldbedoneby came, he danced round her with the others. Then she took him in her arms and cuddled him, and Tom told her that he had never been cuddled before.

"I really will be good," he promised. "I will!"

And for a while Tom did try. But, sad to say, all he could think about were sea-cakes and sea-toffees and all the other nice things locked away in the cupboard that belonged to Mrs Bedonebyasyoudid.

One night, when everybody was asleep, Tom crept away among the rocks to find the cupboard.

When he found it, the doors were open and he thought he might just taste one of the nice things. But after he had eaten one, he ate another and another – gobbling everything up as fast as he could and, though he did not know it, all the time standing close behind him was that strange fairy Mrs Bedonebyasyoudid.

The fairy did not grab him or shake him. She just looked at him sadly. And on Sunday when kind, pretty Mrs Doasyouwouldbedoneby came, she said nothing either. But when Tom asked her for a cuddle, she shook her head.

"I can't," she said, "for you are covered all over with prickles!"

For a whole week poor Tom was very miserable. "Will you take away my horrid prickles?" he asked the old fairy when next he saw her.

"I cannot do that," said the fairy, "but I will bring you a teacher who will teach you how to get rid of them."

Can you guess who she brought? It was the little girl in white – little Ellie!

Tom's new teacher came every day of the week except Sundays, when one of the fairies took her home. After she had been giving Tom lessons for some weeks, he began losing his prickles and Ellie suddenly recognised her pupil.

"I know you!" she cried. "You are the chimney-sweep."

"And I know you!" cried Tom. "You are the little girl in the white bed in the white room," and he laughed aloud.

Then they began telling each other about themselves and Ellie explained how she had fallen off a rock into the water and the fairies had brought her to Tom. Tom longed to give her a hug and a kiss – only he did not dare.

One day Mrs Bedonebyasyoudid told Tom that the time had come for him to go away by himself and see the world.

"You must journey to Shiny Wall," said the fairy, "for there you will find wise old Mother Carey. She is the only one who can direct you to the Other-End-of-Nowhere."

"What shall I find there?" Tom asked.

"Your old master, Mr Grimes," was the answer.

So Tom set out on his adventures and he had so many that they would fill another book if they were all written down.

Perhaps the best one of all was when he came upon a lively little dog that had been shipwrecked. The dog sneezed himself into a water-dog so that he could follow Tom, but it was some strange, jolly birds called mollymocks who finally took Tom and his dog as far as Shiny Wall.

"Dive under the ice floe," they told him. "When you come up again, you will be in Mother Carey's pool," and Tom, not a bit frightened, did just that.

What a large, peaceful pool Tom and his little dog found themselves in. Far away he could see the towering ice cliffs, but of Mother Carey there was no sign. Then he saw that a tall, peaked iceberg was Mother Carey herself. There she sat, without moving, chin resting on one hand, looking down at all the new-born creatures that she had made out of the sea-water. As soon as she saw Tom she asked him what he wanted.

"I am looking for Mr Grimes, the chimney-sweep," he told her, "but it is taking a long time to find him."

"You will find him soon," said Mother Carey, "but don't go yet. Stay and talk to me for it is many years since I had a visit from a water baby."

So Tom stayed and talked to the white marble lady who was as old as the world itself. In return, she told him wonderful stories before sending him on his way.

There is no use pretending that Tom had an easy task finding Mr Grimes, and when he did, he was very sad to see what a state his old master was in. There he was, sticking out of the top of a chimney, his head and shoulders just showing. He was guarded by a fierce truncheon which kept hitting him whenever he grumbled about his unlit pipe.

"I'm glad I found you," Tom began timidly. "You fell in the river, didn't you, and the fairies found you? I expect they could have changed you into a water baby if they had wanted to."

At this Mr Grimes grunted, supposing that Tom had come to laugh at him, but of course he was quite wrong.

"I do wish I could help you," Tom went on earnestly. At this, Mr Grimes began to splutter and cry real tears!

Tom took Mr Grimes to the fairies and they took pity on him. They sent him to sweep the ashes out of the crater of a volcano which was, after all, much better than being stuck fast in a great, tall chimney!

How long Tom had been away on his travels it is hard to say, but in all that time he had not forgotten Ellie, and when he saw her again, he thought she was even more beautiful than before.

"You have grown," said Ellie.
"And so have you!" said Tom.
"One day I'll be a proper man and we'll get married!"
I expect that is just what happened, don't you?

ISBN 978-1-84135-236-7

This edition first published 2003

Published by Award Publications Limited,
The Old Riding School, The Welbeck Estate,
Worksop, Nottinghamshire, S80 3LR

www.awardpublications.co.uk

3 5 7 9 10 8 6 4
08 10 12 14 16 18 20 19 17 15 13 11 09

Printed in China